FLING

A BBW & BILLIONAIRE OFFICE ROMANCE

VIRGINIA SEXTON

LANA LOVE

SUGAR & VICE

For updates on new books, plus exclusive bonus content, from Virginia Sexton and Lana Love, sign up for their mailing list at http://eepurl.com/dh59Xr.

❀ Created with Vellum

SNEAK PEEK!

Up close, I can smell a hint of her perfume and see the remnants of her tan. As I turn to face her, she's looking down at me, a playful smile on her face.

Fuck. Fuck, fuck, fuck.

This is an invitation I can't resist.

"This all looks very good." I stand and move so I'm behind her. "This especially is intriguing," I say quietly, standing so close to her that I can feel her body heat, but not touching her. Slowly, I reach out my arm and lightly brush against hers, then run my finger across her hand and up to her wrist.

"Oh." There's a hint of surprise in her voice, followed by her hips ever-so-lightly pressing back against my cock.

"That might be dangerous, Miss Walker," I say. All I want to do is be dangerous with her.

"Is that so, Mr. Grayson?"

Her voice is a sexy purr, and I can't help myself. I rub against her ass so she can feel just how hard I am for her. She pushes back against me, her hands on the top of my desk.

"Are you sure?" I ask, molding my body against her back and running my hands from her hips and up to her full and perfect tits. She leans into me, and the week on the island rushes back – the sexy way she'd wiggle, whether or not she was above or below me; how ticklish she was just after coming and would giggle at the slightest touch; the lusty smile…

Fuck. She's looking over her shoulder and giving me that smile right now. Her green eyes glint at me as she looks at me over her shoulder and treats me once again to that lusty smile.

"Oh, I'm very," she rubs her perfect ass against me, "very sure."

"Stand up," I demand, pulling her up with me, her body pressed against mine.

I take a short step back and cup her ass in my hands, then quickly undo the zipper and yank her skirt and panties down to her knees. As if reading my mind, she leans over my desk, pushing her ripe, full ass up for me.

The sight of her gorgeous ass and her pussy peeking out at me? I nearly come before I even have a chance to undo my belt buckle. I push my pants and boxers down, and my thick cock springs free.

"Goddamn." My fingers slide along her pussy and come back deliciously slick, and I groan in anticipation of plunging into her.

Allie looks back over her shoulder at me, her eyes glazed as she bites her lip.

"Please," she whispers…

CHAPTER 1

ALLIE

 "Ugh." I flop back onto the clothes piled up on my bed. For me, unpacking meant holding my tattered backpack upside down and dumping everything out. "There's sand everywhere!"

Tara comes into my bedroom and laughs. "Girl, didn't I say let's go to the laundry room and do it? Let maintenance clean up the sand and just dump everything in the washers right away?"

"I know," I sigh, then roll over. "It's just hard to be home, you know. I mean, we knew we were coming home, but... everything is so grey."

"That's called cement, my dear," Tara laughs, plopping down next to me.

"I know," I mime a scowl, but I laugh when I see the face she's making. "Remind me why we had to leave the beach?"

"Because we aren't rich, and we need to work, and our student loans start coming due in a few months? Those diplomas we just received were pretty damn expensive. Or are you just mooning over Stud and finally hooking up with someone? I absolutely can't believe you waited so long! That place was *swimming* with hot men."

Before we knew his name, Stud was the name we gave Colby. He was built like a statue in an Italian museum – all chiseled facial features and a washboard stomach that just begs to be touched. Tara and I had both clocked him checking me out, but I never imagined he'd been waiting around for a chance with me. I'm not like the high-end, high-maintenance women that were a dime a dozen at that resort. Men like him don't go for curvy girls like me.

Or so I thought.

I lay back and close my eyes, remembering Colby. The earthy scent of his cologne comes back to me first, then the perfection of his body and, most of all, the way he knew how to use it. And his hands. And, oh God, his mouth. My body trembles as I remember what he did with his mouth.

"Girl, do I need to leave you alone for a bit?" Tara teases, and I open my eyes. "You look ready to shoot off on the Orgasm Express there…"

My hand flies up to my face, and my cheeks flood with a blush. "I… Man, that week with Colby was something else. I sure wouldn't have minded an entire month, or more, in bed with him!"

"He was definitely fine. I never thought you'd actually be so bold to go over and talk to him! You've never done that before."

"Yeah," I giggle, "that was definitely the first time I picked up a man! He was so…" I pause and try to find the right word, "so experienced. He was definitely in a different league than the guys I've been with, not that I've even been with that many."

"Wasn't he a little older?"

"Only a few years older than us. Tara, I swear on my new job, I've never seen such a perfect body. Oh. *My*. God."

"You're going to have to…"

"No! I will most certainly not tell you the details!" I sit up and grab a pillow, holding it against my stomach.

Tara smiles at me, and I know I don't need to say anything more. We have that level of best-friendship where we really know and understand each other, and we don't have to detail every little thing.

"Your face is going to freeze like that, you know," I joke, poking her in the arm.

"Oh, I know how to perk you up. Shopping!"

Tara jumps up from the bed and pulls my hand so I have no choice but to follow her.

"We just got back…"

"And we both need new clothes for our new, corporate jobs. I know your parents bought you some suits, but we need mix-and-match stuff, too. I'm not sure we'll actually have to wear suits all the time. I mean, that seems so, I don't know…eighties or nineties!"

"Well, fine. I'll go with you. But I'm definitely wearing suits the first week. You know I'm gunning for a full Project Manager job within six months, even though they say it's crazy. I didn't study my ass off for nothing. I've got student loans to pay!"

"Ugh. Don't remind me!" Tara grabs her purse and heads toward the door. "Now let's go!"

~

"Do we really have to wear this stuff?" I ask as we flip through the clothes racks. The sales staff have been eyeing us suspiciously since we arrived, as we're still wearing cut-off jeans and strappy tank tops. Well, Tara is wearing a tank top. I pulled on a lightweight cotton shirt to hide my upper arms. It was one thing on the beach to not worry about how much skin I was showing, but back in the city? I'm reminded of my curves and that I should really be covering myself up.

"We'll get used to it soon. Hey, what do you think about this?"

I look at the cross-over, emerald green blouse Tara is holding up, and I swoon.

"That is the most gorgeous thing I've seen here! Do they have it big enough for...?" I ask, glancing down at my chest. It's always hard to find clothes that fit over my boobs.

Tara's smile drops a little, and I know the answer. *Of course, they don't.*

"You should still try it, okay?"

It's not even that I'm that big. I've never understood why designers don't make more larger sizes or why some of them insist on sizing their clothes tiny enough for a grasshopper. Women are curvy, but so many designers conveniently over-look that, like only Skinny Minnies deserve gorgeous clothes.

"Oh, damn it all." I look in the mirror. The emerald green sets off the tan of my skin like it was made for me. But. There's always a but... The front of the blouse strains over my chest. Miraculously, it fits everywhere else, including the tops of my arms, but even with a minimizer bra, there's no way I could wear this to work.

"Let me look." Tara knocks on the dressing room door.

"See." I will the tears pricking my eyes to not fall. "It's so perfect, otherwise." I don't even have to point at my boobs for Tara to know. I've been through this so many times, it's ridiculous. At least in college, I could wear knits all the time.

"That color looks incredible on you!"

"Thanks. I really, really wish it fit."

Tara's voice softens. "I know. I bet the next store will have something perfect for you!"

"I'd hug you if I wasn't worried about busting out of this

top," I say, smiling at Tara. She always tells me how beautiful and perfect I am, but it's hard when ninety-nine percent of celebrities are all rail thin. Even though I eat healthy, I'm still what Tara calls 'lusciously curvy.' She says she's jealous of my hourglass figure. Times like now, I'd give anything to swap my curves for her boyish figure.

I close the door to my little dressing room and look in the mirror for a long, last look at myself and this blouse. If I can find another blouse I love as much as this one, that would be perfect. It's so much easier to feel confident when I'm wearing great clothes. I often feel like I have to do everything just that little much better or be that little bit more prepared, because my weight and body are different enough to be notable. So many times, people look at me and don't take me seriously, so I know without a doubt that I have to dress absolutely perfectly when I show up at EH Consulting next week. Even though I know I have the brains, I expect it will take some work to convince my new boss.

When I'm stripped down to my underwear, I take another look at my reflection and run my hands over the tops of my breasts, where there are a couple of love bites lingering from my last night with Colby. His eyes held no hesitation when he undressed me and saw me naked, and for a moment, I felt desired and like I didn't need to hide my body or ask him to turn the lights out before we got into bed. Running my hands over my skin, I remember how Colby explored and teased me.

My nipples perk out against my lace bra, and I try to push Colby from my mind. I know it was a vacation fling, but it felt like so much more than just sex. But I know that's just me imagining things.

"Hey! You almost ready in there? We have more stores to hit!" Tara bangs on the door.

I giggle as I shout, "Coming!" I came so often with Colby, I truly lost count.

I never wanted to leave Grand Cayman. Or Colby.

CHAPTER 2

COLBY

*R*andall grunts as he smashes the tennis ball towards the corner of the court I'm *not* standing in. I sprint over and extend my arm in a wild swing to try and return the ball, but I don't make it in time.

"Goddamn, man!" I retrieve the ball and wipe my forehead as I head to the back of the court before taunting Randall. "What's gotten into you? Did you lose a deal this morning?"

"Shut the fuck up, Colby. You know I don't lose. Unlike you, today." He serves the ball so hard it looks like a round, lime-green missile headed straight for me.

I easily return the ball, and we spend the next twenty minutes finishing our set. I up my game and rack up the points.

"Nice turnaround, there," Randall concedes, slapping me on the back. "I thought that trip to the islands made you soft…"

"You have no idea how wrong you are," I say, closing my eyes for a moment and remembering the gorgeous girl I met there. It was a long overdue vacation, and I'd planned on just relaxing on my own. Then I met Allie.

"Oh, really now?" Randall says, opening his locker and dumping his sweaty clothes and gear in his bag.

We both slam our lockers shut and head to the showers.

"Oh, hell yeah, really. This woman was a goddess among women, Randall. Gorgeous, smart, lush body. Good goddamn."

"It's about time you got back on the horse," Randall says, soaping up a couple of showers away. "You've been pissy since that thing with…"

"Don't fucking mention her name," I warn, shaking my head.

Thoughts of Sienna are not what I want in my head. What I want, and who I want back in my goddamned bed, is Allie. Her playful smile and unabashed enthusiasm were exactly the tonic I needed to unwind, not to mention she was sexually confident and athletic. She seemed so shy when I first saw her, but man, once she opened up… I was a fucking goner.

I shake my head again, this time to clear my thoughts of Allie – not because I want to, but because I can already feel my cock stirring, and this is not the place for the raging hard-on even the memory of Allie inspires.

"Peace, dude. Didn't mean to hit a nerve," Randall throws up his hands in a gesture of semi-surrender. "It's been a few years, is what I'm saying. It's not natural for guys like us to be single. Unless you're hiding it, I don't think you've even touched another woman in a while.

"Randall," I warn. He's not exactly non-confrontational at the best of times, and this is not something I'm remotely interested in discussing. He has this idea that being rich and single means all the pussy in the city is a free-for-all buffet, and that he's going to sample as much as he possibly can.

Me? I'm a relationship guy, but after Sienna...I've had no interest in opening myself up to anyone.

"Dude. Forget I even mentioned it."

"Done."

Randall heads out of the showers, grabs a towel, and aggressively dries off. For once, he really does seem sincere. I've told Randall before about how I want to cash out and leave the rat race behind. He thought I just needed a vacation, which I did, but even after two weeks on the island, I still feel the same way about work and giving it all up. There's more than enough money in my portfolio for me to do anything and everything I want, for a few lifetimes over. Enough is enough.

"So what's on the agenda this week? Cracking the whip on the minions?"

I button up my shirt and reach for my diamond cuff links.

"Pretty much. We've got a PR firm coming in to help us with the branding on GrayShield."

"How's the product development going on that?"

"Pretty good, though R&D is behind schedule. Again. I don't know what I have to do to light a fire under those engineers, but they need to step it up. The PR firm can't brand a non-existent product. The shareholders are expecting something groundbreaking and fat earnings next quarter. If we don't deliver, we're up shit creek."

"Man, I hear you." Randall closes his locker and grabs his gym bag. "Lunch?"

I glance at my Rolex Yacht Master and shake my head. "Margie will order something for me. I've got a meeting in fifteen. Another time."

EVEN AFTER A WEEK of the beach and sex with the unforgettable Allie, the tension bunches in my shoulders as I walk through the busy lunchtime crowd of the city.

Just the passing thought of Allie makes my cock strain for her. It was refreshing to be with a woman who didn't know who I am and who wasn't entranced by my bank account. Not to mention that sex with her was fucking stupendous. The way she approached everything with gusto, not just sex, but enjoying food, having fun, always being up for an adventure? It made me want more from her. She was a bit shy at first, but she quickly opened up and was definitely not afraid to stand up to me if she disagreed about something.

As I WALK into the towering skyscraper that is home for Grayson Technology, I look around. Could I give this all up, retire early, and go live on an island like I've been dreaming about, spending my days snorkeling or sailing or eating fried fish?

If I had a woman like Allie at my side?

Absofuckinglutely.

CHAPTER 3

ALLIE

"Hold the elevator!" Elizabeth yells, breaking into a run. Even in four-inch heels and a narrow skirt, she can move faster than an Olympic sprinter.

I jog after my boss, not understanding why we can't just wait for the next elevator. We're early for our meeting, and I really don't see how one or two minutes will make a difference.

We squeeze into the crowded elevator, and the doors finally close. Elizabeth's been talking non-stop since we left the office – she'd call it coaching, but I'd call it pedantic lecturing – making sure I'm ready for what will be my first client pitch where I'll be acting as the lead. I'm a mix of confident and crazy-nervous, not to mention excited as hell.

We're pitching Grayson Technology, Inc. so that we can hopefully land what would be a huge, very lucrative contract to develop the branding for a hush-hush software product they're about to launch. We had to sign lengthy NDAs and basically swear on our future *grand*children's lives that we wouldn't even mumble the name of the product in our sleep.

Plus, they took our cell phones before they would let us in to see a software demo.

Frankly, I think that's a bit ridiculous. I mean, it's just software, right? But, client wishes are client wishes, and I have no problems with following them. While I don't think the software they're working on sounds like a big deal, I had enough business classes in college to know that their competitors would, and that technology moves so fast that losing even a month can mean the difference between success and failure.

I move to the side to let some people off the elevator, and my knees buckle as I catch a whiff of a familiar scent. I'm dead-certain it's the same cologne as Colby wore. Memories of lazy days and the most spectacular sex I've ever had wash over me, and I have to shake my head. Now is not the time to get lost in sex fantasies.

I start mentally reciting the opening of my presentation to clear the memory of Colby's taut abs, the way his blue eyes crinkled with laughter when I'd tickle him, the way he'd then pin me to the bed and tease me mercilessly for having tickled him…

"You okay?" Elizabeth leans toward me, her eyes flashing with panic.

"What? Oh, I'm fine. Just clearing my head." It's better for her to think I'm nervous about the presentation, which I am, instead of knowing I'm fantasizing about the sexiest man I've ever laid eyes on and remembering the spectacular vacation romance I had.

Yeah, *that's* not a story I'm going to tell my boss right before going into a major client pitch.

The door pings, and we make our way to the reception desk staffed by a woman who looks like she makes more money than I do.

"EH Consulting, here to see Mr. Grayson and Mr.

Browning." Elizabeth flicks her straightened blonde hair, and I sigh inwardly as I watch her try to establish dominance over the receptionist. I've seen her do this with other people, not to mention to me. I think it's rude and then I remind myself I'm not going to work for Elizabeth forever. She's really good at what she does, and her consulting firm is well-regarded, so for what feels like the millionth time, I bite my tongue as I stand next to her.

"Ah, there you are," the receptionist says, flicking her brunette hair as she looks up from her computer. "I'll let Mr. Grayson's assistant know you're here, and she'll come out to take you back. You can have a seat while you wait."

Elizabeth is already turning and walking towards the seats, her skinny body slicing through the air of the reception area.

"Thanks," I say, hefting my portfolio bag as I follow Elizabeth and sit down.

Elizabeth turns in her seat to face me and talks quietly. "Okay, just to be clear, you did all your research on Global Tech, right?"

"Yes," I say, frustrated she still doesn't trust me. It's not like I've given her a reason not to. "I researched this company when I was job searching, and I considered a job here. But I heard Grayson is a..." I briefly pause and try to think of something more appropriate than 'total hardass,' which is what every single report of working for Grayson described, "...that he's challenging and demanding."

Elizabeth laughs a little, and her lips break into an unexpected smile.

"That is entirely true. I've been trying to get Global Tech as an ongoing client for the past year and Grayson is, as you so kindly described, difficult. More people call him a ruthless asshole."

For a brief second, we smile and share a moment, which is pretty rare. It makes me feel better about today.

An exceptionally well-dressed woman comes into the lobby. "Ms. Henderson? If you two will come with me."

∾

"AND SO, that's what EH Consulting is prepared to do for Global Technology, Inc. Are there any questions?" I look around the room at the group of ten that I've been speaking to for the past thirty minutes. My presentation has gone even better than I hoped, and I've nailed every question I've been asked so far. The mysterious Grayson has been absent, and I can't say I've been upset by that.

A couple of the men look at each other, and each shake their heads.

"No, Miss Walker. You've been incredibly thorough, and I think I speak on behalf of everyone here when I say you've done an excellent job. We're intrigued. Frankly, your presentation covered points that others haven't discussed, and your insight is top notch."

"Thank you." Outwardly, I smile. Inwardly, I'm dancing around and whooping and hollering from sheer adrenaline and excitement. *My first big presentation is a smash hit!*

"That's fabulous," Elizabeth says, coming to stand by me at the front of the conference room. "We look forward to hearing from you. And please, let us know if you have additional questions or concerns that we can answer."

"We'll take this to Grayson. Expect to hear from us soon."

"You'll take what to me?"

I'm startled at the new voice, for a couple of reasons. One, I never heard a door open. Two, it sounds vaguely familiar and–

Ho. Ly. Shit.

When I look to the new voice, the smile on my face freezes, and my body does that pressure-drop thing, like cresting a rollercoaster peak and then hurtling to what feels like imminent death. The man who's just walked in has piercing blue eyes, high cheekbones, white-blond hair, and a body I have used as a personal jungle gym.

Even in a fine suit and with his blond hair slicked back, there's no mistaking Colby. He still has a hint of a tan from when we were together on the island.

My nipples tighten, and every nerve ending in my body electrifies at just the sight of him. Alarm bells clang in my head, and I don't know whether to run over and jump on him, or to run out of the room. I have no freaking idea how to handle this situation. Do I admit we've met? Or that I want to strip off his clothes and lick him from head to toe?

"Colby Grayson," he says, firmly grasping and shaking my hand.

"Allie...um. Allison Walker."

"Mr. Grayson. How *are* you?" Elizabeth purrs, reaching out a manicured hand and touching his arm.

"Elizabeth," Colby says, his voice cool as he glances to her.

When he returns his gaze to me, he stares right into my eyes, and my skin burns. Surely, he recognizes me? But the look in his blue eyes is inscrutable, and I can't tell if he's trying to pretend that he doesn't.

My stomach tightens. What if I was nothing more than a casual vacation fuck, who he flattered into feeling so special? I mean, it's not like I ever expected I'd see him again, but now that he's here standing in front of me? My brain clouds in a heady rush of emotions.

"Miss Walker gave an impressive presentation, Grayson," Mr. Browning says, coming over. "She really knows what she's talking about and addressed issues no one else has."

"Has she now?" There's a glint in his eye, and I know immediately that he recognizes me, too.

"She's my rising star," Elizabeth says, angling her body so she's closer to Colby.

What the hell is going on here?

Colby turns to me. "Could you stay a few extra minutes and summarize your presentation for me?"

"We'd be happy to." Elizabeth is smiling so broadly it looks like her face is going to crack.

"No. No need for you to stay, Elizabeth. I know you're busy. I won't keep Miss Walker for long."

"Of course." The disappointment in her voice is obvious. She's not the type of woman that is refused very often. "Allie?"

"No problem." It's hard to keep my voice even and professional. "I'm happy to bring you up to speed."

"Good. Please come with me."

CHAPTER 4

COLBY

*T*his is a really bad idea.

I shouldn't be inviting this woman back to my office, just the two of us. Alone.

Fuck.

But I can't help myself. I've been fantasizing about her since I've been home. Back on the island, she had a rule about no last names and no work talk, which was frustrating since I've been fantasizing about finding the girl I spent the most amazing week of my life with and have ached to see again, even if just for ten minutes.

She walks silently beside me as we head to my office. Holding the door open for her, my cock twitches as I watch how her pencil skirt hugs her ass. I'm hard as a fucking steel pipe, and I want to see her naked on my desk.

I settle in behind my desk and take a long look at her. She's perched on the edge of her seat, as if she's ready to take flight at any moment. To Allie's credit, she meets my eyes with her own and doesn't shy away from me.

If I thought she was hot and sexy running around the beach in cut-off jean shorts and a skimpy tank top, it's nothing to how she looks in a silk blouse, pencil skirt, and heels. Goddamn, the memory of her full tits over me as I lay beneath her…I cough and shift in my chair.

I try, and fail, to not stare at her tits. As much as I want to remove whatever is holding her hair up and watch it fall around her face and down past her shoulders, I push those feelings aside.

"So what questions can I answer?" Allie slips into a professional demeanor and sits up slightly straighter in her chair. "Would you like me to give the full presentation? A shortened version?"

"A short version is adequate. I trust my team, and they were clearly quite impressed."

She nods and then launches into a short speech about the brand strategy she pitched to my team. It is, indeed, insightful and thorough.

"That's very impressive," I say when she finishes. "Can you show me what you're thinking of?"

"Sure, just a moment."

Allie leans over to reach into her bag, and I catch my breath as I glimpse the lacy edge of her bra, delicately pressed against her lush tits.

"Okay," she comes around to my side of the desk, an iPad in hand. "May I?"

"What? Oh, yes," I say, moving some files out of her way.

She taps her iPad and brings up a series of files.

"Now, here," she says, pointing to a graph and pushing the iPad so it's in front of me. "Here is the new target demo I discussed. If you look here—" she points at a graph.

Up close, I can smell a hint of her perfume and see the remnants of her tan. As I turn to face her, she's looking down at me, a playful smile on her face.

Fuck. Fuck, fuck, fuck.

This is an invitation I can't resist.

"This all looks very good." I stand and move so I'm behind her. "This especially is intriguing," I say quietly, standing so close to her that I can feel her body heat, but not touching her. Slowly, I reach out my arm and lightly brush against hers, then run my finger across her hand and up to her wrist.

"Oh." There's a hint of surprise in her voice, followed by her hips ever-so-lightly pressing back against my cock.

"That might be dangerous, Miss Walker," I say. All I want to do is be dangerous with her.

"Is that so, Mr. Grayson?"

Her voice is a sexy purr, and I can't help myself. I rub against her ass so she can feel just how hard I am for her. She pushes back against me, her hands on the top of my desk.

"Are you sure?" I ask, molding my body against her back and running my hands from her hips and up to her full and perfect tits. She leans into me, and the week on the island rushes back – the sexy way she'd wiggle, whether or not she was above or below me; how ticklish she was just after coming and would giggle at the slightest touch; the lusty smile…

Fuck. She's looking over her shoulder and giving me that smile right now. Her green eyes glint at me as she looks at me over her shoulder and treats me once again to that lusty smile.

"Oh, I'm very," she rubs her perfect ass against me, "very sure."

"Stand up," I demand, pulling her up with me, her body pressed against mine.

I take a short step back and cup her ass in my hands, then quickly undo the zipper and yank her skirt and panties down to her knees. As if reading my mind, she leans over my desk, pushing her ripe, full ass up for me.

The sight of her gorgeous ass and her pussy peeking out at me? I nearly come before I even have a chance to undo my belt buckle. I push my pants and boxers down, and my thick cock springs free.

"Goddamn." My fingers slide along her pussy and come back deliciously slick, and I groan in anticipation of plunging into her.

Allie looks back over her shoulder at me, her eyes glazed as she bites her lip.

"Please," she whispers, working her sweet pussy over my fingers.

Without a second thought, I plunge my cock deep inside her. I nearly black out from how good it feels to be balls deep in her pussy again.

Oh, God. How I've missed her...

Allie gasps and works her hips as I slide in and out of her, fast. I know I won't last long, and I recognize the way she's shivering – she won't last long, either. Placing my hands on her hips, I guide her body as I thrust faster and faster into her, my cock so hard it hurts.

"Fuck, you feel so good!"

With a delicate moan, Allie's body bucks against me, hard, as her pussy clenches and she comes. Watching her creamy ass sets me off, and then I'm ramming my thick cock deep into her until I come so hard that I'm blinded by the pleasure.

A moment later, I slide out of her and pull up my pants, and she stands up and adjusts her clothes.

An awkwardness descends between us as she turns to face me, her face and chest beautifully flushed.

My body is still thrumming from my orgasm, but my mind is now racing. Do I need to go into damage control mode? I don't *think* so, because she's not some intern...and it's not like we haven't done this before.

"I..." For once in my life, I'm at a loss for words.

"It's fine." Allie runs her hand through her dark curls, and

I exhale in relief. "This is just a one-off thing, right? We're both adults."

"Absolutely."

We walk across the expanse of my office, and I fight the urge to grab her and take her again, this time with her on top, so I can watch her lush body move over mine. I mentally shake my head, willing the new hard-on in my pants to go away.

I open the door for her and hold it open. "That all sounds good."

"Is there anything else?"

"No. No, that will be all. My team will handle all of this."

And just like that, she walks away as if it were the end of a normal business meeting.

Dammit. What have I just done?

CHAPTER 5

ALLIE

"M ake it a double," I tell the bartender at The Cellar, desperate for the vodka tonic she's pouring. I need this drink, in addition to probably one or, let's face it, three more, never mind that it's a Tuesday. The past ten days have been insane, and it's not like I wasn't working all weekend, either. Tonight will be worth the hangover I'll have tomorrow.

"Put that phone down now!" Tara pulls me into a hug. "I'm so happy to see you! It seems like forever since we caught up!"

"I know!" I toss my phone in my purse and take a long drink of my cocktail. "Boy, do I have some news for you. Get a drink, and I'll find a booth."

"Oooh! Intrigue!" Tara laughs, dramatically rubbing her hands together in front of her face.

I smile and laugh. It *has* been too long since we saw each other, but our schedules have been near-impossible to cooperate. Seeing her already relieves the tension that's been burrowed inside me and threatening to give me a migraine.

"This place is sure posh," Tara says, sliding into the booth and running her hand across the starched white tablecloth.

"Yeah, it's nice. My boss brought me here last week, and I fell in love with the place. It reminds me of a swank place from fifties Vegas. Plus, it's pretty quiet, and the booths are private."

"Uh-oh," Tara says, brushing her blonde hair back from her face. "What's wrong? Is your boss being a slave driver?"

"Oh, she's been fine. I nailed the presentation for Global Tech, and she's been fawning over me ever since, especially since the CEO wanted to speak to me privately, and apparently he raved about me."

"Oooh, look at you! Getting in with the top brass! Good job!"

"It gets better. Or worse. Dammit, I don't know what I've gotten myself into." I suck down the rest of my drink. "Do you remember that I considered interviewing at Global Tech?"

"Sure. I don't remember why you didn't, though."

"Rumor had it that the top boss is a total hard ass. Remember?"

"Oh, yeah! I remember now. Weren't they your top choice?"

"Yeah, they were definitely my top choice. But the stories about the CEO made my skin crawl. Ruthless. Demanding."

"Yessss. Is he giving you a hard time? Is he a fat, old geezer?"

It feels good when I laugh. There's been way too much stress and not enough laughter recently.

"Oh, Tara, my darling. He is everything *but* an old, fat geezer. He's hot as fuck and more handsome than you would believe." I can't help but smile. "Actually, you *would* believe how handsome he is. Remember Stud?"

Tara is silent as she watches me, and then a light clicks on in her eyes.

"Shut the front door! There's… No way!"

"Yes way," I confirm. "Grayson and Stud? They are one and the very same."

A low whistle escapes from Tara's lips, and she shakes her head in amusement. She waves for a waiter. "Another round, please." Turning to me, she adds, "And now I see why you're drinking doubles. Holy hell, woman. How's it going? Did you…"

"Umm…"

"Allie Walker! You didn't!" Tara's eyes are wide and trained on me.

I wring my hands, pushing them into my lap.

I lower my voice as I start to speak. "Um, yeah. We may or may not have fucked in his office when I gave him the summary of my presentation. I feel like I've made this terrible mistake, but I just couldn't resist, you know? I stood next to him to show him something on the iPad and…he was behind me, and my skirt came off."

"Whoa. Drink up," Tara says as our fresh drinks are placed before us.

"Part of me thinks I need to tell Elizabeth, even though I know that's a horrifically bad idea. Do you think I need to tell her? I don't even know how to have that conversation!"

"Oh, hell no. The correct answer is that you absolutely *do not* have that conversation. Ever." Tara takes a long drink from her cocktail, her eyes watching me closely. "How did you not realize he was the client you were pitching today?"

"Remember the rules I laid down? No last names, no real-world talk? And I was so busy preparing my presentation, I never looked at the About page of their website, where I would have seen his photo. I don't know what I would have done if I had known! Should I start looking for a new job?" I wring my hands again. This project *is* the kind of high-profile project that anyone would kill to have on their resume, and I really don't want to give it up.

"Honestly, Allie, just keep your head down, do the work, then move on. I mean, is anything really going to happen between you two?"

"Yeah, you're probably right. I have no idea. Besides, men like him don't date women like me." I sigh, looking down at my drink. "They all date models that look like stick insects."

"Allie," Tara says, her voice low with warning. "You know you're gorgeous. Didn't he already prove to you that he thinks you're sexy and desirable?"

"Sure, but that was vacation sex and last week was... I dunno. A really bad decision? We've all done things on vacation that we wouldn't do in real life. You know that. What about you and that Danish guy?"

Tara narrows her blue eyes at me. "Allison Walker. You did *not* just invoke Jesper. We do not talk of Jesper, I don't care how many vodka tonics you've had. And do not try to change the subject!" More gently, she says, "I know you're sometimes self-conscious about your curves, but you are way more sexy than you realize. Seriously. Tell me you remember that?"

"I do," I say, my voice tiny. "It's just that old insecurity. I mean, we had such a great time on vacation, and he really did make me feel like I was the only woman in the world. I can't envision he would want something more from me."

"Maybe he does..."

"Tara. Stop it right now. That's a fairy tale, and I'm way too old to still believe in those. Besides, I don't care what you say, but he's so far out of my league, it's not even funny. It was just, I dunno, a random office fuck? Oh, Tara! What have I done?"

"I think you've gone and done what most women aren't

even brave enough to fantasize about. Just play it cool." Tara downs the rest of her drink and sucks one of the ice cubes. "Maybe just try going with it? I still think… no, I *know*, you can have any man you want."

"Thanks, Tara. It just doesn't feel like that some days, you know?"

"I do."

I love her for saying this, even though I don't believe her.

As I GET ready for bed, I stand naked in front of my mirror and look at my body. Even though *I* think I'm pretty, I don't feel like most men can see anything other than the extra curves I have. Still, I smile when I see the tan lines I still have and remember how much Colby loved to trace them with his tongue. He'd drive me crazy, because he'd take so long to thoroughly enjoy my tan lines.

I should put Colby out of my mind. It's not like anything is going to happen again.

But how am I supposed to work with him?

CHAPTER 6

I knew it was a bad idea to suggest dinner with Allie tonight. Even with the guise of it being a working dinner, which it has been, there's no denying that every time we look at each other, we're clearly thinking about how I bent her over my desk and fucked her, and imagining each other naked, again. And sweating. And moaning. And, goddamn, I've been battling a hard-on all night.

"So, I think this plan will really help you reach the next level with your marketing for GrayShield. Reaching the college market is critical," Allie says, intent on the report next to her on the table. Her dark curls are escaping from whatever is holding her hair up, and I have to resist reaching out and tucking that hair behind her ear and running my fingertips over her skin.

"Are you even listening?" Allie says, a playful smile quirking up her mouth.

"My apologies." I really do need to calm myself before we stand up and leave – even though I don't want the evening to end.

Allie and Elizabeth have been working with my in-house team for a few weeks now, and the ideas they've brought in, mostly thanks to Allie, have been remarkable. Their work on refining the brand for GrayShield has been excellent.

Allie sits across the table, swirling the beer in her glass as she watches me. Her green eyes meet mine, and I love the challenge I see in them. Most women play along to what they hope I like, simpering and fawning over me. I prefer an intelligent woman who isn't afraid to challenge me.

"Look. Maybe we should go back to the office to discuss this a little more," I say, smiling at her.

She sits back in her chair, and the way her silk blouse clearly clings to her gorgeous breasts is downright obscene.

Fuck. I need to fuck her again...and not quickly. I need to watch her moan, to watch how she gasps as I plunge my dick into her and fill her up so completely that she deliciously squirms against me. The voice in my head that is yelling this is dangerous? I ignore it. Of course, we can keep this casual – just another fling.

"That... I'm not sure that's entirely the best idea." When she crosses her arms under her chest and pushes her magnificent tits up, I know she's game.

"I don't know what you're thinking." I grin at her. "I just think it would be more... comfortable, than this restaurant."

Chang's is a great Chinese place, but the lights are bright, and the colors are too sharp. A dimmed office, the lights of the city twinkling in the windows? That is much more the ambience I want to share with Allie right now.

"So, you're saying you think it would be better—" Allie leans forward and rests her arms on the table, her cleavage now an enticing tease in front of me "—or perhaps more productive, to take this professional discussion somewhere...quieter?"

I lean forward, maintaining her gaze. "I do. I most certainly do."

"Well, if you absolutely insist." A wicked smile curves on her lips. "I can be persuaded. There is still more to review and discuss."

We walk the five blocks back to the office in silence. Her hand occasionally brushes mine, and I want to pull her into a dark doorway and kiss her so long and thoroughly that we both forget our names. Instead, we walk down the street, playing at respectable.

"Watch out!" I say, turning and wrapping my arm around her waist and pulling her to safety as a dirty yellow taxi speeds through a red light and through where she had just stepped. "Are you okay?"

Allie turns her body to me, her eyes wide in surprise and fear, her body trembling. She bites her lip and nods, as if what just happened doesn't quite compute.

Seeing this vulnerability and having just saved her life? All at once, the rest of the world falls away. I want to protect her. I also want to fuck her. *Again.* I know this is a bad idea. She's one of my consultants. Fucking your consultants is certainly not a good business decision.

But.

I haven't been able to get her out of my mind since we met, and now that she's in my life again? She's fucking irresistible. Maybe we can just have a little fun. More fun fucking, then we go our own ways. We're both adults.

But.

When her green eyes look up at me, I'm pretty sure she's not a woman I can just have some fun with and leave behind. I start to pull back, but then she's pressing her body into mine, tilting her head up.

"Thanks for that." She recovers her composure, and her breath puffs on my neck, the faint scent of her perfume tickling at my nose. I want to investigate her body, very closely, to find exactly where she has applied it. I slide my hand so that it's resting on her hip and again, she pushes into me.

"You are very dangerous. You know that, right?" I can hear how thick my voice is, and with how close we're standing, I'm sure she can feel how much my cock wants her, too.

"I have absolutely no idea what you're talking about," she teases, lifting a hand to my chest and pressing slightly so that I step back. "You've just saved me from imminent death. Or a broken leg. Isn't this where I say 'and how can I *ever* repay you'?"

"The light's green." I cough and take another step back.

This is such a bad idea.

But I can't say no – especially when we get to my building and she bumps into me; I nearly come when I feel her full breasts lightly press against my arm.

"Evening, George." I nod at the evening security guard in my building.

"Just about to do my rounds. Mind if I join you in the elevator up?"

"Not at all."

In the elevator, we all ride up quietly, though the air feels supercharged and electric. She runs her finger along the outside of my hand, and it's a delicious tease. Not being able to touch her is an exquisite torture. I focus on the display showing the floors the elevator is rapidly passing, counting down until we're on my floor and I can strip her clothes from her, touch and taste her body again.

"Don't work too late, now."

"We'll try not to be too late." Allie flashes George a big smile. "Just a couple of…details to take care of."

I let her walk in front of me, happy that I'm now free to openly stare at her. Her ass sways as she walks, and I want to personally thank whomever it was that designed the pencil skirt.

"About GrayShield..." Allie's voice is almost a whisper as she pushes the door closed behind me. I reach to the top button of her blouse, and the wicked smile reappears on her lips.

"Oh, no. Mr. Grayson," she teases, taking a step back from me. "I don't think that's...appropriate."

I growl, every cell of my body desperate for release.

"I disagree, Miss Walker. I feel it's very appropriate." I take a step closer to her, but she takes two steps backward, maintaining a frustrating distance between our bodies.

The sound of her laughter makes me smile. She extends her hand to me and leads me to my chair behind my desk, then pushes me so I'm seated.

"Mr. Grayson, I feel compelled to say that there are basic ground rules, if we pursue this—" her eyes glance away for a moment before returning to mine "—arrangement."

"Oh really, Miss Walker? Please share."

She holds up her finger. "No sleepovers. No dates. No expectations. No strings."

Even with the amused and sexy look on her face, her green eyes make it clear she's serious.

"That all sounds reasonable. Terms accepted."

"Good. Now, no touching. Remember that." She smiles and turns away from me, swaying her hips as she walks toward the floor-to-ceiling window.

"How about some music?"

I pick up an iPad from my desk and tap it. "Any requests?"

"Whatever you were last listening to."

"You might want to rethink that..."

"Unless it's one of those business self-help gurus, which doesn't seem your style, any music is fine."

A few taps of the screen later, and the sound of steel

drums fills the room. It is the music of the islands, and I've had it on constant rotation since I came home. The music makes me happy and reminds me of where I wish I still was.

"Really?" A smile quirks Allie's lips as she looks at me.

"Yes," I say, suddenly feeling self-conscious. "This is what I've been listening to when I need to get in the zone and work through difficult problems. It helps me focus on where I want to be." I open and close my mouth as she starts dancing in the light, rhythmically moving her body to the music that's coming from the hidden speakers.

"You really did like the island life, didn't you?"

"I did. Very much so. That wasn't a ploy to get you to like me." I spread my legs as I watch her start to move, her body swaying. "One day, hopefully sooner than later, I'm going to retire and buy a house on the beach."

Allie shakes her hips, and I rub my cock through my pants. It's aching and straining to be released.

"That doesn't sound like a bad plan." She raises her arms above her head, and it takes my breath away. She's curvy as fuck and sexy as hell when she moves her body. And oh, does she know how to move her body! I know Randall and other friends of mine prefer women who look like underfed models, but I love how Allie's body is rich and supple. She's gorgeous and radiant.

"It wouldn't be bad if you joined me…" I know this is dangerous water to be treading in, but I can't help it. She seemed so at home on the island, as if she felt as comfortable and happy there as I did.

Allie wags her finger at me in admonishment, though there's a smile on her face.

"Mr. Grayson. Tut, tut. As lovely as that sounds, I'm not looking for a relationship. And that sounds like a very 'relationship' thing to even bring up. Remember the rules: this is casual – nothing more."

I bow my head, trying to hide the rush of disappointment I feel. *But what were you expecting?* I wasn't looking for one, either, but Allie is making me rethink that. Whenever I see her, I want to spend more time with her.

"You know you're an incredible woman, right?"

She's untucked her blouse and is slowly unbuttoning it, from the bottom. When she's undone about half of the buttons, she stops and dances some more, her arms again raised above her head.

"I'm glad you think so." Allie shimmies are turns, shaking her glorious ass in my direction.

I loosen my pants and free my cock, stroking it slowly as I watch her dance to the music. She moves like a mermaid dancing in the waves to the tropical sound of the steel drums. Over the course of two songs, she removes all of her clothes, so she's dancing naked across from me, her hands cupping her breasts and pushing them up.

Goddamn I want to bury my face in her tits. "Let me see how you touch yourself," I demand, grabbing my cock and pointing it toward her. "Show me what you do when you're alone and think of me."

She almost stumbles as she turns slightly away from me, then she looks at me over her shoulder, a slow smile spreading across her face. "Only if you show me, too."

I suppress a growl and stroke myself, this time with more force. There's no way I'm going to be able to delay coming like a rocket.

The music flows around me, and watching Allie, for a moment I forget where we are. She dances slowly, running her hands over her body, pinching her nipples and leaning her head back as she shudders slightly. She lowers herself to her knees then slowly crawls a foot towards me, her green eyes locked on mine.

I wrap my fingers around the tip of my cock, stroking

myself in time to the music. Allie sits up so she's kneeling in front of me, licks two of her fingers, and plunges them into her pussy.

Her breath hitches and speeds up as she plays with her pussy with one hand, her other hand roaming over her creamy tits, massaging them and playing with her dusky nipples. More quickly than I would have imagined, her body starts to tremble, a little cry escapes from her mouth, and her body is jerking. Allie bears down on her fingers, pressing her legs together, riding out her orgasm. I recognize the glazed look of delight in her eyes. My own fingers work up and down my cock, and I can already feel my orgasm surging through my body and ready to burst.

When she lifts her glistening fingers to her mouth and licks them slowly, one by one, my orgasm breaks free, and I grunt as my come shoots out of me. A bit lands on Allie's breasts, and when she reaches down and rubs it into her skin, I swear I nearly come all over again.

No one has ever made me come like this without touching me. This woman is magic.

CHAPTER 7

ALLIE

I want to go home and drink an entire bottle of wine.

Today has been the day from hell. Elizabeth is on a rampage because we're behind schedule. Is it my fault? Not in the slightest. But even though it was someone on the Global Tech team that made the mistake, *I'm* the one paying for it since I'm the one who's in front of Elizabeth.

The pants of her suit swish slightly as she paces around the conference room. I try to be as quiet as possible, even though I want to stand up to her and tell her that now I'm not getting any work done, because she expects me to nod and say the appropriate 'you're so right' every time she stops talking long enough to breathe. She's run her hand through her blonde hair so often and aggressively, it's a wonder she still has any left on her head.

"Oh, and another thing," Elizabeth says, pausing mid-tirade about the 'fuck up of epic proportions.' "I saw you and Grayson at dinner the other night. Looked like you were trying to get cozy with him. Don't."

Oh, hell. I can't figure out what's going on with Colby.

Well, massive chemistry and sex is what's been happening. But that's not something I'm ever going to tell Elizabeth about. I'm not suicidal.

"We were just working late and grabbed dinner. We had a few laughs, sure, but we were back in the office and working right after."

I mentally cross my fingers at that. Yes, we were back in his office, but unless you count performing a strip tease and watching your client jack himself off as you do, work...then, no, we were not working when we went back to his office.

"Allie, please. I'm a woman, and I have eyes. You were totally mooning over Grayson. I understand – he's undeniably sexy. He's also notoriously single and hasn't even dated in years."

She stops moving for a moment and closes her eyes, an unexpected smile moving across her mouth as she obviously fantasizes about him. Listening to her go on about how she is eventually going to land him is like listening to a broken record – one that I've been listening to for the last few weeks.

I don't actually know what is going on between Colby and I. There is something between us, even though we've carefully labelled it as 'just sex.'

"It's not like that," I say when I realize I've fallen into my own reverie, and her eyes are slicing into me like lasers.

"Riiiight," she responds, shaking her head as if I was a child obviously lying to her. "Look, I really don't care if you fantasize about him all night long. Just don't let this crush of yours affect your work. He's out of your league. Besides, eventually he's going to realize how we'd make an amazing team, and he'll finally stop declining my invitations to... expand our relationship from that of a professional one."

Puh-leeze.

I focus on my PowerPoint presentation and tune out Elizabeth as she goes on about how she and Colby would be a match made in heaven. She thinks he could propel her company and career and makes it sound like that is what's more important to her. It's obvious she's also attracted to him, but it never sounds like she knows anything about him, other than his corporate assets and potential to help her career.

"Are you paying attention?"

My eyes snap up, and I realize I've just ignored something I should have actually been listening to.

Dammit. Giving her ammunition to be upset with me is the last thing I need right now.

"I was just reviewing this…"

We both turn at the sound of a knock on the conference room door.

"Yes?" Elizabeth calls out, annoyance unhidden from her voice.

"I just wanted to check in and see how everything was coming along."

My heart flutters as Colby steps into the conference room. Just the sight of him releases tension in my neck and makes me feel better.

"Of course, of course." Elizabeth's icy attitude drops as she puts her elbows on the cherry-finish conference table and leans forward, pushing her arms together to showcase her breasts. Colby barely glances at her. "What can we do for you?" Her voice comes out softer and more like a purr, a tone she never uses when she talks to me.

"I need some reassurance that everything is going as planned, that there won't be any hitches or delays."

As he says this, his forehead creases in stress, and I find myself wanting to get up and wrap my arms around him and give him a huge hug.

What the? My mind races at this. When did I start feeling

more for him? This is supposed to be a fling, which is my rule, not his. He's hinted at wanting more, and he's been asking me to spend the night at his place, but I'm still scared he'll break my heart.

"Oh, everything is going as planned," Elizabeth lies. I turn my head quickly to her, and she shoots me a sharp look that carries a clear warning to keep my mouth shut about the difficulties she was just ranting about. "Is there something specific you would like me to explain?"

Colby turns his blue eyes to me, and an urgent rush of desire shoots straight between my legs, soaking my panties instantly. I clench my legs together, trying to avoid thinking about how delicious and perfect it feels when he touches me down there, when he kisses me down there, when he...

"Allie," Elizabeth's voice has a sharp edge back to it. "Are you listening? Can you pull up the ad campaign Mr. Grayson just asked about?"

"Oh, yes, yes. Sorry." I say, looking down and hoping neither of them notices the flush on my face. I switch screens and open the brand document he wants to see. "So, as you can see, this is where we're at with the branding." I point to the screen, then turn to Colby.

"Just a moment." He pulls a chair over to me and leans in so close I can smell his cologne. I bite my lip as he smiles at me, then says, "Please continue."

I force a cough so I can have a moment to collect myself. Colby's knee is pushing at mine beneath the table, and shivers tickle over my skin.

"We're just awaiting confirmation on these three assets here, but I expect to have those by lunch tomorrow."

I will myself not to look him in the eye, in case I lose all ability to talk while Elizabeth is in the room. Colby is close enough that his body heat warms my bare arm, and all I can think of is peeling his fitted suit off his perfect body and riding him until I can't stand up straight.

"This all looks excellent, Allie. Thank you for your fine work on this," Colby says, his breath puffing against my cheek as he leans in. "Can you explain this," he leans closer, stretching his arm inches from my breasts, and points to a graphic on my laptop screen.

"Oh. Yes. Do you remember that new market I mentioned? Targeting college students? That's what that is. It's a slightly different look, more targeted to that demo-graphic."

"Ah, yes. Good. Good. For someone just out of college, you are incredibly astute and talented."

"She is good, isn't she?"

When I glance at Elizabeth, her eyes are seething with jealousy and suspicion.

"Oh, thanks. I don't think it's that difficult," I say, even though Elizabeth originally tried to shoot this idea down, and it took a couple of days for me to convince her to give it a go. Her precise words were: *It's on your head if it backfires.*

"Don't sell yourself short." Colby pushes his chair back and moves to stand up. "Your insight is an incredible asset, and I'm thankful you're working on this project." His smile cuts straight through the haze of my lustful feelings and natural insecurity, and I realize he really means this and that he's not just subtly flirting with me. Okay, he might be flirting with me, too, but he's not saying this just to make me feel good. He's saying it because he believes it.

"Well, thank you, Mr. Grayson. I'm really happy you're confident in my work."

"Oh," he says, his mouth quirking into a playful smile, "I'm very happy with you."

At this, I can't stop the blush that rapidly spreads across my face.

CHAPTER 8

COLBY

*D*ude, you are wound up," Randall says loudly enough that I move my phone away from my ear. "You need to go out and fuck a chick. Lucky for you, that's what I had on the agenda for tonight, so we can tag team."

I lean back in my leather office chair and spin around to look out the floor-to-ceiling window.

"Randall, I'm going to pass," I say, a frustrated sigh escaping my lips. There's one girl I want to fu... no, I don't want to fuck Allie. She's worth more than that and besides, she's getting under my skin.

"What the hell, bro? I remember the days you never said no."

"Well, let tonight be the first time," I say, clipping my tone. Randall's my best friend, but he wouldn't get it. He didn't get it when I dated Sienna, and he won't get it now. He thinks settling down is for chumps and has gone as far as to get himself neutered so some woman doesn't 'accidentally' forget to take her birth control or contact him and claim he's the father of her child.

"Have you… Are you dating someone? Is there something you're not telling me?"

There's a sting in his voice, which if I'm honest, is fully justified. I haven't been talking to Randall. As much as I've tried to treat this thing with Allie as an extension of the fling we had on Grand Cayman, I know it's something different. She's compelling and sexy, and every time I'm with her, I want so much more. I want to know about her childhood, the secrets she doesn't tell her best friend. I want to bring her breakfast in bed and then have morning sex with her.

"Randall, no. Come on," I say, feeling bad at how I'm not telling the full truth. "You know I'd tell you if there was someone.

"I don't know, Colby. You've been really cagey lately. It's not like you."

I exhale a deep breath. "Well, maybe there is someone I've been seeing, if you can call it that. I like her, but we've both been treating it as a fling, since she's busy and I need to focus on GrayShield. You know what I'm working towards. And you know how these launches are – a never-ending stream of details. And if I don't review it, I won't feel confident that everything is taken care of. You know how I am."

"Yeah, okay." Randall doesn't sound convinced, but he's not pushing the matter further, which is good. He may be my best friend, but there are things he just doesn't understand and which I can't really talk to him about. Allie is top of that list right now. Not because he wouldn't believe me, but that he wouldn't believe I'm honestly ready and willing to pursue something more serious than a few hours of superficial companionship and enthusiastic, but ultimately forgettable, sex with a woman I'll never see again.

I end the call and toss my phone back on my desk before turning back to the window. The lights of the cars are brighter now, everyone rushing to be somewhere.

I wish I was rushing to see Allie.

A DISCREET KNOCK at my door breaks my reverie. Instead of getting down to the details of the upcoming launch, my mind keeps wandering back to Allie. The way she smiles, the way her curves feel in my hands and against my body, the way she tastes...

"Sir. Do you need anything else tonight?" Margie asks, standing in the doorway to my office.

"No, that's fine. I've got everything covered. Go and enjoy your evening."

"If you're sure. Thank you."

I nod and watch her close the door behind her. Margie is an excellent executive assistant. She's astute and quick, she knows how to be unobtrusive, and she's not shy about working hard and getting the work done. I don't know where I'd be without her, and I strive not to be overbearing or unreasonable, even though I know I have a tough reputation.

Once the door is closed behind her, I pull at the knot of my tie and undo the top buttons of my bespoke dress shirt. I'm up and heading toward the deluxe bathroom in my office, and I strip off my suit in record time while I wait for the shower to heat up.

The hot water sluices over me, and I lower my hand to my throbbing cock, gripping it tightly. Now, I let my mind wander back to Allie, the softness of her skin, her sensuous curves, and the enthusiasm she has when we have sex like hormone-fueled teenagers. One of my favorite memories is her above me while she held my hands down above my head, and the sounds she made as I sucked her nipple and pounded my cock up into her as she ground down onto me. She is most definitely not shy about how much she enjoys sex and physical pleasure.

One hand against the shower wall, I brace myself as I work my fist fast and hard over my cock, unable to slow down and savor the fantasy. My body starts to quake and rumble, and then I'm coming hard and powerfully, imagining that instead of shooting my load into the water, I'm spraying my seed across Allie's luscious tits as she kneels before me.

"Fuuuuck," I yell, twitching as I finish coming.

By the time I'm back at my desk, I'm determined to avoid her as much as possible, if not entirely. I want her, but I remind myself she doesn't do relationships. Fuck if that doesn't make me want her even more.

I think about our recent conversation about what was going on between the two of us. *I'm not looking for a relationship,* she said. *Me, neither,* I said, though I knew it was a lie the moment the words crossed my lips. *A relationship would be a bad idea. Contractor. Boss. You know what I mean.* I'd agreed, though I said what I thought I should, not what I wanted to say. I wanted to say *You. I want you.* Goddamn if Allie doesn't have me second-guessing myself and wanting to trail her around like a lovesick teenager.

What woman doesn't do relationships?

CHAPTER 9

ALLIE

I should be working.

There are so many details to keep track of right now, it's hard for me to turn off the work part of my mind and enjoy this party Tara's dragged me to. I've had a couple of glasses of wine, but everyone is grouped together chatting, and it reminds me of being in high school and watching all the popular kids in their exclusive cliques.

"Why are you hiding out over here?"

"There you are!" I turn to her, grateful that she's back. "I didn't know where you went."

Tara tucks a few strands of blonde hair behind her ear.

"Wait. You're not quite so put together as you were when we arrived? Were you…?"

"Maybe." She grins like a maniac and continues to smooth her hair. She nods at a hunky guy across the room who's animatedly talking to some other hunky guys. "You see him, with the good hair?"

"Damn, Tara! Did you know him?"

"No! Totally met him in the bedroom when I was dropping off my jacket."

Of course, she did! I envy Tara and how at ease she is with herself and how quickly hooking up with a guy at a party is so effortless and natural for her.

"You are a force of nature, you know that, right?"

Tara grins at me and gives me a big hug. "Oh! There's Priya. I've been trying to get a hold of her for a week! Catch you later?"

I laugh and nod my head, watching as Tara sashays across the living room and successfully captures the attention of the guy she just hooked up with.

"Hey. Mind if I join you?"

When I turn to the voice, I'm confronted with a guy who looks like he just stepped from one of those catalogs filled with ridiculously expensive preppy clothing.

"Sure." I'm not really interested in hooking up with anyone, but I'm not foolish enough to say no if a good-looking guy wants to chat me up.

"I'm Josh. How do you know Bailey and Kristin?" He nods in the direction of the couple hosting the party.

"Oh, they're actually better friends with my best friend, Tara. I've only met them in passing a couple of times. Honestly," I say, taking a drink from my glass of wine, "I've been working a ton lately, and Tara insisted I come so I could let off some steam."

"They do throw good parties. Your friend is smart."

"Yeah. What about you?" Even though this is pretty basic conversation, at least it's a nice change of pace from the 'so what do you do' that most people tend to ask first thing.

Josh tells me how he met Bailey when they were both competing for captain of the rowing team. "It was all-out war, I tell you. Bailey probably would have made coxswain, but he broke his leg and had to sit out for the rest of the year."

We chat for a while longer, the conversation flowing

easily. He's better than most men about not staring at my cleavage. It's a refreshing change to talk to someone who's more mature than most guys my age. Normally, he's the kind of guy I'd be interested in – handsome, a gentleman, funny. He tells me a string of funny stories, and it feels great to laugh and not think about work for a little while.

And it certainly doesn't hurt that several girls are staring at me and him, clearly jealous he's talking to me and not them. I stand up a little straighter, feeling proud and buoyed by being the sole recipient of his attention.

I hear Josh gasp, and I turn to him. "Are you okay?"

"What? Yeah. I'm fine." He puts down his glass of wine on a side table and smooths back his hair. "Do you know her?"

I follow his gaze, and he's staring at Sadie, a gorgeous redhead – creamy skin and slender, soft curves. I didn't know her well in college, but we saw each other around and were more than passing acquaintances.

"Sadie? Sure, I know her."

"Whoa," Josh looks at me, his eyes wide in admiration. "Could you introduce me? I've been wanting to meet her, but I've been too chicken to talk to her."

Say what?

I drain the rest of my wine while I count to five and try to calm myself down. Even telling myself I shouldn't be upset because I'm not interested in him doesn't work to stop me from shaking in embarrassment and rage.

I've only been a fill-in conversational partner. It's not like he actually wanted to talk to *me* or to ask *me* out on a date.

Once again, I feel like the odd one out. Of course, I was foolish enough to think this guy was politely trying to chat me up. But, no, he was just talking to me while he waited for a *slender* girl to walk in.

"Oh," I say, backtracking. "I don't really know her that well. Haven't seen her since college, really." Doesn't matter that was only a matter of months ago, but I'm not going to tell him that.

"Please, Allie?" Josh is practically begging now, and I feel my shoulders tighten from stress.

This sums up so much of how it was for me in college – always being *The Friend* or *The Girl Who Can Introduce You To The Hot Girl*. I want to run and hide, not because I wanted anything from Josh, but because it felt nice to think a guy was chatting to me because he was interested.

"I… um… She likes strong men. You wouldn't stand a chance." I marvel at how confident I sound and how I didn't just fold and go into 'sigh, fine, I'll introduce you' mode, like I would have in college. It hits me that being with Colby, even though it's just a fling, that I feel more confident about myself.

I walk away quickly, weaving through the now-crowded living room as I make my way to the kitchen.

"Goddamn it all," I mutter, my hands shaking from fury as I empty the last of a bottle of Malbec into my glass then uncork another. I should have just stayed home and got ahead with work.

Carefully carrying my wine, I head back into the living room and look around for Tara. There were a few people I recognized when I arrived, but they all seem to have disappeared, and now everyone that's still here is huddled in cliqueish groups.

"Are you really sure about that?"

I glance at the two mini brownies on my napkin and then up at an over-tanned, skinny blonde woman. She and her friends don't even try to hide how they're trying to make me feel bad.

"I mean," one of the blonde's friends say, "that dress already looks a bit…tight. You might want to lay off the desserts. You're not going to get a guy looking like that."

Just like that, my anger level goes through the roof. A voice in my head says 'yeah, you would die to know who I've been having sex with,' but I don't actually voice the words. It took me a long time, but I stopped trying to justify myself to mean girls like these. They wouldn't believe me, anyway.

I walk away from them and head straight to the bedroom to pick up my jacket. I have no idea where Tara is, but I'm not staying here any longer. A party sounded like a great idea, but I don't fit in here. Maybe I've been naïve, but I thought everything would stop being so superficial once we graduated from college. I know I shouldn't let girls like that get to me anymore, but after what happened with Josh, it just felt like salt being rubbed in a wound of self-doubt.

Sorry to bail, T. I'm headed home. Talk tomorrow. xoxo

MY HEELS CLATTER to the floor before my front door even closes behind me, and I immediately get out of my party clothes and change into my pajamas.

Even after another glass of wine, the sharp remarks of those girls from the party keep crowding my mind. I want to go to sleep, but I can't quiet my head, and tension is creeping in little knots in my body.

I wish Colby was here.

Whoa. What?

Now that he's in my head, I can't get him out.

I stretch out on my couch and run my hand across my breasts and feel how perked out my nipples are already, just at the thought of Colby. Sliding my hand down my body and into my pajama bottoms, I push my fingers into my folds and marvel at how wet I am. My clit pulses as I tease it and I imagine that it's Colby touching me, his mouth hovering over my sex as if he's about to eat me out. I rhythmically stroke two fingers across my clit, and my body turns molten as my orgasm builds.

Imagining Colby's blond head between my legs, his tongue sucking and licking at me, I clench my thighs and cry out as my orgasm floods through my body.

CHAPTER 10

COLBY

This launch is going to be the end of me.

I'm listening to my team make excuses about why things are behind schedule, and I want to fire every goddamn one of them. They're talented, sure. But making deadlines? This isn't the first time they've cut it close. I know they'll get the job done, but I'm going to need blood pressure medicine by the time it's done.

Closing my eyes for several moments, I visualize being at the beach, hopefully Allie by my side, no electronics in sight.

"Okay. How are we going to address these programming issues? Launch is days away, and we can't roll out a buggy piece of shit software. QA was supposed to have gone over this with a fine-tooth comb, and everything was supposed to be fixed." I look around the conference room, and only one person will even pretend to meet my eyes. Heads are going to roll when this is over, and they know it. "Who dropped the ball?"

A hush falls over the room with the only sound that of people nervously shifting in their seats. Finishing this software and getting ready for launch has been extremely diffi-

53

cult, for avoidable reasons, and their fear of pink slips being handed out are not unfounded. If GrayShield isn't ready by launch, there will be several job openings on these teams.

"It wasn't…"

"Speak up," I demand, turning my attention to Browning.

Browning clears his throat and continues. "It wasn't one person. QA missed something, and then programming made changes after, which QA didn't get a chance to test thoroughly, and…"

I interrupt him. "That sounds like a long string of excuses. What's being done to address these issues and ensure we have a product at launch? You all can goddamn well be sure that you will be fucking begging our half-ass wannabe competitors for a job if GrayShield isn't perfect and launched on time."

The room falls silent again, and I have to work to control my rage and frustration.

"Dev is working on ironing out the bugs as we speak," Dora Baldwin speaks up. Her hands flutter as she speaks. She opens her laptop and types rapidly. "Look," she says, more confidently now. "Dev already has the bug fixes in production, and they should be implemented within the next hour. Barring any additional…"

"There will be no more 'additional' bugs, do you understand?"

Dora blinks rapidly and nods. "Yes, sir, Mr. Grayson."

"Get back to work, everyone. I expect progress reports first thing in the morning, and I expect it to be good news. If you don't have significant progress to report, expect to be fired."

I CAN FEEL my blood pressure rising as I think of all the

problems with GrayShield right now. It's a relief when my phone rings.

"Hey man, how you doing? You free?" Randall asks, the cacophony of a crowd coming through the phone.

"I wish. Where you at?"

"Just left a fucking investor meeting. You know that lot I want over on forty-fifth? Some asshole has a hard-on for the building and doesn't want it torn down – and I can't push forward on the deal without unanimous approval. I'm walking back to the office right now. I need some space before dealing with anyone else. Everyone and their fucking uncle is out here today."

"That's tough, Randall. You still going to chase the deal?"

"You bet your ass I am. That's prime motherfucking real estate."

I tap the icon for speakerphone and put my phone on my desk as Randall launches on a litany of how he's going to win over the reluctant board member.

"But I'm up for beating your ass at tennis on Thursday. You free?"

I smile at his cocky self-assurance. "I should be. We'll see about whether or not you win again. I'll have my own frustrations to work out. This launch is a never-ending string of fuckups. It'll be good to have all this behind me."

"Not this talk about running away to an island and sitting on a beach. Don't you know how *bored* you'd get?" His voice snaps with exasperation. He still thinks I'm having a mid-life crisis, no matter that I'm not close to middle aged.

"I'm sure I could keep myself occupied." Like a heat-seeking missile, my hand moves to my groin, and I'm already half-stiff thinking about the beach and Allie. If I had her at my side, I'd never be bored. I wouldn't want to sleep just so I could spend more time with her.

There's a whoosh, and the background noise fades to

nothing. "Right. Catch you later. I'm at my building now. Gotta figure out how to win this deal."

"See ya."

THE KEYCARD READER emits a muted beep, then my private elevator smoothly and silently rises to the fiftieth floor. I do love my penthouse, though for the first time in a long time, it feels empty with just me in it. Despite paying through the nose for an interior decorator, it looks like a showroom. *This place doesn't feel like home.*

I pour three fingers of Irish whiskey in a glass and stretch out on my vintage Chesterfield couch. The burn of the whiskey feels good going down. Thinking about Allie, I pull my iPad from my briefcase.

A slideshow of pictures of Allie on the beach scroll past my screen. Her wonderful dark, curly hair flying in the wind; her smile and laughter showing nothing but pure joy. There is only one picture of the two of us, and it's the one I look at the longest. We were out on a boat for a snorkeling trip, and we're sitting together, drinking those rum punch drinks you can't avoid down in the Caribbean. Her hand is on my knee, even though she's looking away from me. Her friend who snapped the picture caught the unabashed desire on my face as I looked at Allie.

Even when we met, I knew there was something special about her. She had insisted then, as she does now, that what's between us is nothing more than a fling. Of course, that was easy to believe then, because she declared personal information off limits. Yet the way she has her hand on my leg, as if she's making sure I'm still there and as if I'm *hers*? I want to be hers. And I want her to be mine.

Finding a woman that's intelligent, engaging, and sexier than hell? That wasn't supposed to happen.

Fuck.

She's the biggest challenge I've ever faced and I can't, and won't, back down. I need to figure out how to demolish the wall she has around her. The GrayShield launch is coming up, and I dread that I won't see her regularly again, or that she'll declare our fling finished and walk out of my life. I've always been the one who was in control, steered relationships. With Allie, I've lost control, and it's driving me crazy. I want to fall asleep with her, wake up with her, have her as the one person in my life I know I can always count on.

I want to give her the world.

I have to win her over.

I'm in love with her.

CHAPTER 11

ALLIE

*H**ot damn.*
     I give myself a fox whistle when I see my reflection. Turning in the tiny dressing room, I keep my eyes on the mirror and marvel at how this is an off-the-rack dress. It hugs all the curves I want emphasized and downplays the curves I want minimized. In short, it's the perfect dress.

Except it's electric blue.

A knock on the door and Tara's voice interrupts my conflicted thoughts.

"How's it going in there? Can I see?"

"I'm decent." I unlock the door and step out into the hall.

Tara's eyes go wide, and she makes a 'turn around' gesture with her hand.

"Damn, girl! You look gorgeous! That dress is painted on."

"Isn't it? And the top of the dress actually fits my breasts, and the whole thing is amazingly comfortable!"

"It's a show stopper, that's for sure. Can you afford it?"

"Yeah, but I should buy the other dress I was looking at. I don't think this one is right."

"What do you mean? I've never seen a dress that looks so perfect for anyone! I mean, seriously now, that looks like it was designed especially for you. What's not to love about it?"

Tara's eyes are wide in disbelief. I can't blame her, and I certainly don't disagree with her.

"It's the color." I step back into the dressing room and look at myself in the mirror again. "Shouldn't I be wearing a little black dress? That's what every other woman there is likely to be wearing. It's like the tuxedo for women – you just put it on, put on some jewelry, and you're done."

"Allie," Tara's voice is firm. "That's exactly why you should buy *this* dress, instead. You want to stand out in the crowd. Don't blend in!"

"I don't know." Turning and looking at the back view, I can't get over how amazing this dress makes my ass look. "Do you really think so?"

"I know so. So much so, I'm taking this dress—" she snatches the black dress from the hook it's hanging on "—and I'm going to go hide it. Allison Walker, you are buying that dress, and that's final!"

Tara has a grin on her face, and it makes me laugh.

Running my hand down the sides of the dress and facing the mirror, I can't deny how gorgeous the dress is.

"Okay, you've convinced me. But now I have to find a new pair of shoes – I don't think I have any that match this."

Tara throws her arm across her forehead and leans backwards dramatically. "Shoe shopping! Oh! No! The horror of it all! I don't know how I'll ever survive!"

I laugh and swat at her arm. "Stop it! We can go to Winston's after and share a slice of that German Chocolate cake and have some wine."

"Well, when you put it *that* way…"

～

A T W INSTON'S, we've polished off the cake and nearly a bottle of wine between us.

"So, what's going on with you and your boss these days?"

"Elizabeth? Oh, she's just the usual pain in the—"

"Girl, you know that's not who I mean. I'm talking about Stud!"

My cheeks color.

"Oooh, so you've slept with him...*yet again*, hmmm?"

Tara leans forward, her blue eyes intent on me.

Glancing around Winston's, which on a Saturday afternoon is pretty busy, it seems everyone is engrossed in their own conversations.

"Well, yes, we have." I look away, a rush of warmth flooding my core as I think about the strip tease I gave Colby. It was so much fun, and I felt like a complete sexy babe, which isn't something I've felt often with other men. With Colby, it feels like he sees beyond my exterior and he really likes *me*.

Yet the idea of trying to explore something more with him terrifies me. What if he's just like all the other men I've dated and everything falls apart when we attempt to make it 'real'?

Tara leans back slightly and cocks her head. "You really like him, don't you?"

I meet her eyes and nod. "I do. The last time we were... together, it felt different. It wasn't just a hookup, and it wasn't just sex. There was something more there. At least, it felt that way to me." I look away and sigh, the pleasure of the memory deflating a little. "But you know me. It's not like I'm good at judging men, so I'm probably mistaken entirely. Would he still like me if we weren't just sleeping together?"

"Allie." Tara's voice is firm. "Look at me. *I've* seen the way he looks at you and the way you two were together back on

61

Grand Cayman. Even then, it looked like something more than casual. Don't sell yourself short."

"Tara, I'm not."

"Allie, yes you are, and you need to stop it. You're gorgeous, smart, and you're a couple of years from being at the top of your game, professionally speaking. You are now and always will be an incredible catch. I wish you really understood that."

I bite my lip. I know Tara is right, even though I don't always believe it. Being a little extra curvy – just that little bit different – usually has people doubting me, thinking that I'm less than what I say I am or thinking I'm capable of less than what I can really do. Even though, generally speaking, I'm reasonably confident about who I am and my abilities, I'm still always battling that little voice that says 'no, those people are right… you're not good enough.' When it's in a professional setting, it's easier to brush these thoughts aside, because I know deep down that I can do my job and do it really well. Yet when it comes to a man, I have no self-confidence that they see me as anything more than a passing conquest.

"Thanks, Tara." I take a deep breath and try to calm the burst of emotions that are threatening to spill tears down my face. "I know you're right, it's just so hard. It certainly doesn't feel like 'just sex' anymore, but I'm so scared to even consider that there might really be something there. I mean, me and Colby?"

"Again, don't sell yourself short!" Little blotches of color rise in Tara's cheeks, and I can see how frustrated and angry she is.

"I'm not! It's just…look, I'm so far from his world, right? You were with me when we Googled his exes. I don't care what you say, but I'm not the same league as them, or him."

"Well, at least just have fun with him. You've been going

on about how you don't want a relationship of any kind until you're more settled with your career, and you've said he's not the committing type, so why not just let it be fun?"

Tara catches the eye of our server and motions for the check.

"Now, cheer up. Have fun. You'll find the right guy, I swear it."

In my Uber on the way home, I can't help but wonder what it would be like to be Colby's girlfriend.

As MUCH AS it's true I want to focus on my career, these last couple of weeks with Colby have had me wanting to be in a relationship. The little time we've spent together has reminded me what it's like to have a man in my life. Colby makes me feel special.

And I haven't felt that special in longer than I'd care to admit.

Yet the idea of hoping Colby thinks I'm special, and that there's a chance it could really go somewhere? The idea is incredibly thrilling, and the possibility of being hurt is terrifying. The connection I think and hope is between us? Its stronger and deeper than anything I've felt with anyone else, ever.

Stop it, Allie. You're just a little drunk. Be sensible. I remind myself about my goal to not let myself have any distractions from my career and what Tara said about just enjoying myself and having fun.

My phone dings and a picture pops up, of Colby in bed, a book propped on his chest and his hand on the pillow next to him.

There's a pillow with your name on it. x

I look at the picture, and it sucker punches me in the heart. This is the man I want.

Naughty boy. You know the rules... xxx

Never have I wanted to break my stupid rules more than right now.

CHAPTER 12

I look around the ballroom and see all the people who have come out. The press is hovering and waiting for the chance to interview me or my team. Even though I tried to keep the press out, because they're crazed rabid vultures at the best of times, Elizabeth and Allie advised against it.

Now that GrayShield is finally launching, I'm already planning who my successor will be. Patting my jacket pocket, the printed brochures for property down on one of the smaller Cayman Islands crinkles slightly. I have a couple picked out, and I want to invite Allie to join me. I'm prepared to do whatever it takes, and I'm unwilling to take no as an answer from her.

"Well done, man. It looks like you've got yourself a massive success, here."

I turn and smile at Randall.

"Thanks, man. It's been a slog, and I'm glad it's over." I grab a glass of champagne from a passing waiter, even though it's not something I drink often. I need something to take the edge off my nerves. I don't want whiskey, because I want to be absolutely clear-headed when I see Allie.

"So, what's next for Big Man Grayson?" Randall laughs, slapping me on my shoulder. His eyes are following one of the PR girls who inevitably clog these events, wearing a little black dress, and her straight blonde hair hanging talk down her back. They're interchangeable and forgettable.

"Well, you know…" my voice trails off as I see a flash of color in the distance.

The bright blue of Allie's dress catches my eye, and I marvel at how beautiful it looks on her. In a sea of little black dresses nearly every other woman is wearing, she's a knockout.

"Look. I see someone I have talk to. Catch you later, alright?"

Randall nods, his eyes roaming over the PR girl's unnaturally thin body. "Congratulations. You did well."

"Thanks," I say, but we're both already walking in different directions.

"Mr. Grayson!" A male journalist holds up his phone to record me. "A word or two? I have questions about GrayShield."

"Sorry. Not now." I keep my eye on Allie, not wanting to lose sight of her for even a second. "Or, you can talk to Dora Baldwin. She's the head of Marketing. She's over there," I point to her. As soon as the journalist turns to look, I'm off. I don't care that it's rude. Allie is my only priority right now.

"Colby!"

"Later, please."

I move to Allie as fast as I can, ignoring everyone asking for my attention.

Allie's eyes are wide as she looks at Elizabeth. When I get close, Elizabeth's voice is a low hiss. "That dress is a bit much. You should cover yourself up. You're…abundant for a dress cut like that."

"Actually, Allie's dress is stunning," I say, coming from behind Elizabeth and going over to stand next to Allie. "The dress makes her stand out, which she should, because the work she's done surpassed even my most ambitious expectations. It's refreshing to see a woman with enough imagination to not dress like a clone. Her imagination is what makes her so good at what she does."

Elizabeth looks chastised, and the color drains from her cheeks. Her hands smooth over her black dress, and I can see her struggling to compose herself. "Right. I'm just going to talk to the writer from Tech Review Weekly. I promised him a few minutes."

As we watch her walk away, a luscious giggle escapes from Allie's mouth, and it takes everything in me to not lower my mouth to hers and kiss her deeply…right here, in front of everyone.

"No one *ever* talks to her like that!" The look of pure joy and amusement on her face is worth whatever backlash Elizabeth might try to dole out to me. Not that I plan to be around to accept it.

"Well, maybe people should." This time, I reach out and gently wrap my fingers around hers. Her eyes widen as she glances from me to our hands and back to my face. "You really do look stunning. I love that you chose a vibrant color. You stand out from the crowd, and not just because of that dress. There is no one I'd rather be with tonight, than you."

"Why… Thank you. I'm happy to be with you tonight, too." Allie squeezes my fingers, and my heart thumps wildly in my chest. "The early reviews of GrayShield are wonderful. Congratulations. I'm thrilled for you." Allie smiles, and I'm as gawky and nervous as a teenage schoolboy talking to his first crush for the first time.

"Thank you, Allie."

I reach out and touch her arm, letting my hand linger and trail down toward her hand. I want to leave this party behind, leave all the schmoozing to the PR and marketing teams. Sure, this thing was my brainchild, and I can talk about what it does, but that's not where my mind is tonight.

"Can we talk? Later?"

"Of course. I'll be here."

A light tap on my arm, and I turn to see Margie. "Sir, you're due to give your speech in five minutes. We should get you backstage now."

Dammit. Seeing Allie made me forget everything else about this damn launch. I don't want to be apart from her, even for a minute.

"Don't go anywhere, okay?" I squeeze her fingers as she nods, and her brown curls bounce.

"I wouldn't think of it."

"YOU'RE GOING to wear a hole in the floor if you don't stop pacing," Margie says. "Everything alright?"

"Yes. I just want to get this over and done with. There are...other places I'd rather be right now." Like with Allie, preferably on a sun-drenched island, especially if she's wearing something skimpy, or, hell, nothing at all.

"Hm. With a Miss Walker, I take it?"

I glance quickly at Margie. She's always been a keen observer of people, in addition to treating confidential information as truly confidential.

"To tell the truth, Margie, you're right." There's no reason trying to deny it, especially now that Allie and Elizabeth have finished their contract.

She glances at her watch and then back at me. "Thought

so. You've never had such a junior employee, or contractor, in your office so much. Besides, it's pretty obvious when the two of you are together. If I can say so, it's been a while since… I'm pleased to see you happy again."

"Thank you, Margie. I appreciate that."

"And now," the emcee's voice booms through the sound system, "I'm pleased to introduce the man behind it all, the reason we're here tonight, the mastermind behind Gray-Shield. Put your hands together for Colby Grayson!"

I plaster a smile on my face as I take a step toward the stage.

"Thank you," I say, tapping my headset and moving in front of a screen with the GrayShield logo splashed across it. "And thanks to all of you for being here and supporting this product."

I click through the brief presentation Margie drafted for me, with highlights of GrayShield that we want the media to pick up on, a description of how GrayShield will change the face of privacy for social media users, and why this is important.

"We deserve the right to control our online life. As we know, once something is online, it's there forever. In a world dominated by social media posts, GrayShield allows the user to control their data, in a comprehensive way that no other service offers. GrayShield is unparalleled. It has no competition."

I look out to the hundreds of faces, and the excitement zipping around the room catches up with me. I grin and play to the audience…giving them just enough information to make them want to know more, enough information to make them hungry for need this app, and that they will readily hand over their money.

The color of Allie's dress catches my eye, and I pause. Even with the adrenaline rush of the launch, seeing her reminds me of where I want to be – and that isn't on stage or working at my corporation. I rush through the rest of my speech and then rush off the stage, waving away everyone who wants some of my time.

There's only one person's time I want.

ALLIE'S EYES catch mine as I'm ten feet away, and the smile that lights up her face gives me hope. There's no way she could look that happy to see me if she *only* wanted a casual relationship.

"Let's get out of here." I tug on her hand, nodding in the direction of the lobby. "I have a suite booked."

"Oh, do you now, Mr. Grayson," she teases, a wicked smile on her lips. "I don't know if that would be…professional." Her green eyes twinkle, and she takes a step closer to me.

"Well, as of now, you and Elizabeth are no longer contracted by Global Technology. So that means you and I can do whatever the hell we want to do. Like this."

I pull her close, lower my mouth to hers, and kiss her deeply. Allie moans and kisses me back without inhibition, reaching up and threading her fingers through my hair and pulling my head closer.

The people around us quiet, and when we part from our kiss, breathless and panting; sure enough, I see cameras pointed towards us. *Fuck it. I don't care if we make the gossip columns tomorrow. Allie is worth anything and everything.*

"Well, that sure got everyone's attention," Allie says, suddenly bashful. She wraps her arm around my waist, and I pull her close in a protective gesture. "And yes, let's definitely get out of here."

Without a second thought or goodbye to anyone, I lead

her from the ballroom and across the hotel lobby to the bank of elevators.

"Hold the elevator…" a voice calls out, but I jab the Close Door button.

"We could have waited…"

I push Allie against the wall as the elevator starts its rapid, silent ascent.

"*I* couldn't wait."

I press against Allie and relish how her body feels against mine. I love her delicious and luscious curves.

Her hand slides down my back and grabs my ass, and I groan with passion. Her tongue invades my mouth, bringing a taste of champagne to my tongue. When she moves her hand around and runs it up and down my cock, I nearly explode right there.

Tonight is not a time to rush, so I pull back and just look at her. Allie's eyes are bright, and her breath is uneven as she looks up at me. Looking at her takes my breath away. She's the most beautiful and desirable woman I've ever encountered. Not to mention her sex appeal is off the charts.

"Why did you stop?" She pushes her hips against me, and a primal sound escapes me. *What is it about her that makes me lose all control?*

"I want to savor tonight. To savor you."

CHAPTER 13

ALLIE

*T*here is a discreet click, and the door quietly pops open after Colby swipes a platinum keycard for the Presidential Suite. I gasp when I see what's inside.

The hotel suite Colby leads me into looks like a home, not a hotel room. It's like in those movies, where someone wins big in Vegas and is comped an amazing room. There are three dark-grey couches in a sunken living room area, facing a floor-to-ceiling window that looks out over the twinkling lights of downtown. There are so many chairs and tables around the room, I have no idea what the hotel thinks visitors will actually *do* in here. Maybe hold a business conference? Off to the side, there is a curving staircase leading to some kind of loft.

Walking through the suite, I count no less than five paycheck-busting bouquets of flowers on some of the tables in the room. I come to a stop in front of a pristine floor-to-ceiling window and look out at the landscape of the city at night.

Colby stands about a foot behind me, his blonde hair as bright in the reflection as the lights in the city below us.

Colby.

Confusing emotions swirl through my mind. Despite everything, I thought I could keep up this no-strings charade with him. But... I want more, so much more. Tara has been telling me to talk to Colby, but... I've been chicken.

I have to stifle a gasp as I wonder if this is my last night with Colby. Of course, it must be. I've told him I'm not interested in a relationship, and he agreed it's just been a fling.

Goddammit. How come when I finished college and said I wanted to focus on my career, the perfect man walks into my life? And how come I was foolish enough to keep him at arm's length?

"Hey, Allie. Are you okay?" Colby's arms wrap around me from behind, and his muscular body presses against my back. He holds me, and I let myself lean back into him, pretend for a moment that he's mine and we're just unwinding for the day. The scent of his cologne tickles my nose, and I know this is one of the things I will miss about him.

"Mmm. Yes. It's just been a long week, with the launch and dealing with Elizabeth, you know?" Talking like this, like we're a couple checking in at the end of the day? My heart reels with the desire that this was the reality of our relationship. To blot out the ache I feel in my heart, I turn in his arms and wrap my arms around his waist, trying to pull him a little closer so I can kiss him.

"Look, I know you've made it clear you're not the relationship type, that you've just been having fun. I can't help it, and I understand if you say no, but I want more with you. I want what we have to be the beginning of something great, not just a pleasurable interlude in our lives. I never want you to be a memory."

The look of hesitation and worry that creases Colby's brow makes me pause. Realizing he is serious makes me tremble with excitement and vulnerability. I've barely admitted to myself how much I like him, and I certainly have tried not to let myself hope too much that something real and lasting could build between us.

"Have I gone too far?" Colby's voice is small, betraying his fear.

"No, no," I say, reaching out and touching his arm. "I'm just…surprised. Happily surprised."

Colby puts his hand over mine. "But you've said you don't do relationships, that you wanted to keep everything casual. I don't understand. I'm happy, but confused."

"Well," I take a deep breath. "The truth is, I've always been the relationship type. But, I always end up getting hurt. While I was on Grand Cayman, I first tried to avoid men altogether so I wouldn't meet someone and get hurt. Then you came along. I was attracted to you, and I could tell you were attracted to me. Tara kept telling me to just have a fling, keep it fun and light. Eventually, I couldn't resist trying to talk to you and, well, have some fun. So, I pretended to be someone I'm not…pretended to be the type who didn't let themselves get involved in something serious."

Colby's blue eyes are intent on me, and a dizzying wave of vulnerability forms in a cloud around me. But I've started telling him all this, and I can't stop. If I don't put my heart out there now, I'll never forgive myself.

"But even on vacation, I knew it was different with you, that you were someone I could fall deeply for. Finding out you were a client knocked me for a loop!" I half-laugh at the memory, and Colby smiles, too. "I had no idea what to do, except I knew better than to breathe a word to Elizabeth. She…"

"Yes, she's been after me for about a year now. I know all about that," Colby nods and sighs. "It doesn't make things easy or optimal, but she's very good at what she does. So… sometimes the awkwardness is worth the results."

"And it gave us a second chance."

"That it did; that it did."

A dazzling smile stretches across his mouth, and desire shoots through me.

"I honestly had no idea what to do, but then it was obvious you were interested, too, and to be honest there was no way I could resist you. And I assumed there was no way you could be seriously interested in someone like me. I continued the 'no commitment' charade, because I thought 'okay, let's just be selfish this once, let's just let this run its course and enjoy the ride.' I thought I could get you out of my system, the project would end, and we could go our separate ways…"

"But…" Colby's voice is soft, and he runs his hand through his blond hair.

"But I didn't want to stop. I couldn't stop." I lace my fingers through his and squeeze tightly. "Each time I've been with you, I've wanted it to never be the last time."

"That's how I feel, too," he says, tugging my hand so I move closer to him. The scent of his cologne reaches me, and I find it still makes me shiver. He just smells so right. "I want to always be with you."

My body quavers, and tears of joy start to fill my eyes. "The idea that I'd eventually have to give you up killed me a little. I braced myself that every time was the last time, and then it would be a rollercoaster when it started again."

"Oh, Allie. Honey." Colby wraps his arms around me and holds me so tightly I almost can't breathe. "Allie, baby," he pulls apart from me just enough to look into my eyes. "I love you. I love you for who and how you are, and I would never consider giving you up for anything – not for a moment. I never thought I would fall in love again, but you've shown me I hadn't understood what love was. You're the dream I didn't even know I could hope for."

"Oh, Colby." I gasp as tears roll down my cheeks. "I love you, too. Now and forever."

All of the walls I've been trying to hold up come crumbling down as Colby kisses me, and I let myself finally, fully, feel all the emotions for Colby that I've been trying to ignore. A feeling of safety and security overwhelm me as he holds me tighter, pressing my body against his and intensifying his kiss.

Without breaking our embrace, Colby guides me across the room, his body hot against mine.

"After you." Colby gestures at the spiral staircase, breathless.

"Oh, Mr. Grayson. I'm not sure that's appropriate…" I giggle as Colby swats my ass.

"I'll show you what's appropriate, Miss Walker."

Colby runs his finger under the hem of my dress, pushing it up as his hand moves around my leg. I feel his hands on my hips, and I stop moving. He moves his hands down my body, spreading my thighs apart.

I gasp and grab the handrail as he kisses my legs while sliding one of his hands up to my thigh and into my panties.

"You like that, Miss Walker?"

"Oh, yes, Mr. Grayson." I squirm on his fingers, desire burning through my body. I want…no, I *need* more than his fingers inside me right now. I want to seal our love with my body and soul.

A moan escapes my lips when he pulls his fingers away from my slick folds, but then he's pushing my legs further apart and pushing his tongue into my pussy.

I grab the handrail and try to brace myself. Colby's tongue is forceful, licking and circling and driving me crazy. My clit feels like it's the size of a marble, and it's exquisitely painful how much I need release. The stairs wobble beneath my feet, and suddenly I'm lowering myself to my knees, unable to stand. I grab onto the step in front of me, bracing myself as Colby's tongue continues sucking at me, making my body sing and tremble with pleasure.

"Oh!" My orgasm slams through my body, surprising me with its power. I bear down on Colby's tongue, and he keeps licking at me, more slowly now.

Colby trails a line of kisses down my thigh while rubbing his hands over my ass.

"You taste absolutely amazing."

I grin, looking over my shoulder and watching him lick his smiling lips.

We stumble up the stairs, his hands never leaving my body. It seems like a magic trick how quickly our clothes fall from our bodies as we make our way to the bed.

"I love this tan line," I say, kissing Colby beneath his belly button. His breath quickens as he pushes his hips up toward me.

"I love all of your tan lines," Colby says, breathless. I move my body above his and slide myself down onto his thick cock.

No matter how many times we have sex, the moment he enters me makes my world still and feel complete. I look down into Colby's eyes as I begin moving my hips back and forth and raising my hands to play with my nipples.

"God, you feel so good," Colby moans, putting his hands on my waist and pulling me down to him. My breasts press against his chest as he claims my mouth in a deep, demanding kiss.

Colby guides my hips as I ride him. My body is already shaking again, another orgasm rapidly building and expanding in my body. I raise my head and look into Colby's eyes, and my hair falls down around our faces, creating a space that is just him, just me.

"I'm so close," I moan.

"Come with me!" Colby cries out, holding me tightly and thrusting up into me. I grind my hips down against him, moaning in pleasure as his perfect cock rubs against my spot over and over. A primal sound escapes from Colby's mouth, and I feel his body shake at the same moment my orgasm unleashes. My body bucks against him, trying to fit more of him in me as we come together.

After we catch our breath, we roll over, and Colby puts a pillow under my head. I roll over so we're facing each other, and he wraps his arms around me, holding me tightly against his muscular body.

"I'm never letting you go. I love you, Allie. Come live with me on Grand Cayman. We'll get a little house, go swimming, do nothing or everything. I don't care as long as we're together. Will you marry me?"

Colby reaches under a pillow and pulls out a small, red velvet box. When he opens it, the most beautiful diamond ring I've ever seen glitters and sparkles back at me. I take it from the box and hand it to Colby so he can slide it on my finger.

"Oh, yes! Colby, yes! There's nothing more that I want than to build a life with you. I love you so much."

"You have made me the happiest man in the world, Allie."

Colby slips the ring on my finger then rolls on top of me.

"I think we need to, ahh…seal the deal. What do you think, Miss Walker?"

I grin at Colby, love and lust and excitement rushing through every molecule of my body.

"Well, Mr. Grayson," I say, reaching under the covers, "if you absolutely," I stroke his cock, "positively," I guide his cock between my legs, "insist." Colby slides into me again, slowly, and I arch my back as pleasure takes over my body. "Absolutely."

THANK you so much for reading *"Fling"*!

Are you ready for even more from Virginia and Lana?

For updates on new books, plus exclusive bonus content, from Virginia Sexton and Lana Love, sign up for their mailing list at http://eepurl.com/dh59Xr.

For a full listing of Lana's books, go to her Amazon.com Author page at:

https://www.amazon.com/Lana-Love/e/B078KKRB1T/

For a full listing of Virginia's books, visit her Amazon.com Author page at:

https://www.amazon.com/Virginia-Sexton/e/B074P8YG4F/

If you enjoyed this book, please consider leaving a review on Amazon or Goodreads (https://www.goodreads.com/author/show/18128893.Lana _Love) or BookBub (https://www.bookbub.com/authors/lana-love). Thank you!!

ABOUT VIRGINIA AND LANA

Virginia

Virginia writes the kind of stories she enjoys reading — steamy romances that always end with happily-ever-afters. She loves making an accomplished alpha fall hard for his perfect match, and thinks it's delicious when he must work to win over her heart, while also making her knees go weak and leaving her breathless in all the right ways.

Lana

Lana spent years as a technical writer, before giving in and writing romances like the ones she'd been secretly reading since forever. She loves to write stories that are a little bit flirty and a little bit dirty. Okay, more than a little dirty…

Like Virginia, Lana also loves travelling, and they have gone on some trips together, which may or may not include beach vacations, but which they have sworn each other to secrecy over…

CPSIA information can be obtained
at www.ICGtesting.com
Printed in the USA
BVHW031653140519
548254BV00001B/79/P